THE PUPPY PLACE

BUBBLES AND BOO

THE PUPPY PLACE

**Don't miss any of these
other stories by Ellen Miles!**

THE PUPPY PLACE

BUBBLES AND BOO

ELLEN MILES

SCHOLASTIC INC.

*For all the readers who have written to tell me about
your bunnies!*

Copyright © 2016 by Ellen Miles
Cover art by Tim O'Brien
Original cover design by Steve Scott

ISBN 978-1-338-06900-6

10 9 8 7 6 5 4   17 18 19 20

Printed in the U.S.A.   40
First printing 2016

CHAPTER ONE

"Lizzie, is that you?" Mom called from upstairs.

Lizzie pulled her nose out of the soft fur on her puppy's neck just long enough to answer. "It's me!" she shouted back. Then she went back to kissing Buddy, who had been waiting at the door when she arrived home from school. Buddy greeted her every afternoon, tail wagging and ears perked. He was the cutest, most kissable puppy ever and the best friend anyone could ask for. Lizzie stroked his brown fur and tickled the white heart-shaped patch on his chest. "I wish we could play," she told him, "but you know I have to get going if I'm going to finish before dinner."

1

Lizzie and three of her friends had a dog-walking business that kept them very busy in the afternoon, after school. It was important to Lizzie that every dog on her list got her full attention. She did more than just walk dogs: depending on what her clients wanted, she also fed them, groomed them, and helped train them.

Lizzie Peterson loved dogs. In fact, she was pretty much dog-crazy. She loved to play with dogs, draw them, read about them, and write stories about them. She had even convinced her parents that their family should foster puppies. Being a foster family meant taking care of puppies who needed help. Every puppy who had stayed with the Petersons had stolen Lizzie's heart, but the whole point of fostering was to find them excellent homes. That was why none of them stayed for very long — except for Buddy. He was the one puppy the Petersons had not been able to give up: now Buddy was a member of the family, along with Lizzie and her younger brothers, Charles and the Bean.

Lizzie was still sitting in the front hall, petting Buddy, when her mother walked down the stairs. "Hi, sweetie," Mom said. "On your way out soon? Mrs. Mooney just called to say she didn't need you to stop by today."

"Again?" Lizzie shook her head. "I don't get it. Why wouldn't she want me to take Bubbles for a walk?"

Bubbles was a beautiful standard poodle puppy, just a few months old. Lizzie loved her bright eyes and soft reddish-brown curls and the way she bounced along so eagerly when she and Lizzie walked down the street together. Lately, though, her owner, Mrs. Mooney, kept canceling.

"I don't know why she tells you not to come," Mom said. "You'd think she would welcome your help, with the new baby and all."

The Mooneys' little girl, Aria, was only about a month old. She was cute, with wavy dark hair and wide eyes — but to Lizzie, no baby could ever be as adorable as a puppy.

"Anyway, how about a snack?" Mom asked Lizzie. "You can tell me about your day while you eat."

"No time," Lizzie said. "I'll grab an apple." She kissed Buddy between the ears once more and gave him a squeeze. "We'll play later," she promised him. She did not want Buddy to feel neglected. She stood up and kissed Mom, too, then headed for the kitchen.

Lizzie took an apple from the bowl on the counter and reached for her dog-walking backpack, which hung from a hook near the back door. It was stuffed with things she might need: an extra leash and collar, some treats, a doggy water-bottle, plastic bags, a small first-aid kit, and a stack of index cards with information about each of the dogs she took care of. Lizzie kept very careful notes on her charges; she knew which ones were slowpokes, which ones might not be good around children or other dogs, and which ones needed some extra training on the basics, like sit, come, and heel.

As she walked down the sidewalk toward her first client's house, she sorted through the cards and pulled out the one for Bubbles. Sure enough, according to Lizzie's records, Mrs. Mooney had canceled five times in the past two weeks.

Lizzie thought about it. On the days she had walked the pretty poodle recently, Bubbles had not been so bubbly: she was not quite as prancy or as bright-eyed as usual. She had dawdled on the leash and had not seemed interested in the treats Lizzie offered.

Lizzie knew that Mrs. Mooney was very protective of Bubbles and took excellent care of her. Lizzie was not even allowed to give the puppy any new treats until Mrs. Mooney had read the entire list of ingredients in them and approved it. Lizzie was sure that Mrs. Mooney would have taken Bubbles to the vet if she was sick.

Lizzie's heart beat a little faster. Maybe Bubbles had some terrible disease. Poor Bubbles! She was too young to be dealing with a serious illness. Or maybe it was something else. Maybe the Mooneys just needed to change her diet or give her some supplements to boost her energy.

Lizzie decided to stop at the Mooneys' after she'd taken care of the other dogs on her route. She needed to know what was going on with Bubbles.

First she had dogs to walk. She started with Tank, a German shepherd who was as strong as his name. When Lizzie had first started walking Tank, he was a puller. He would charge down the sidewalk, practically dragging Lizzie along behind him. Over the past few months, he had finally started to learn to heel. Part of it was the new no-pull harness Lizzie had convinced his owners to buy, and part of it was all the training she had done with him. Now Tank would walk nicely by her side — unless, of course, he spotted a squirrel.

Next she walked Dottie, a sweet Dalmatian who was almost completely deaf. Lizzie had worked with Dottie, too, teaching her hand signals. After Dottie were Maxx, the energetic miniature Doberman pinscher, and Scruffy, the adorable dust mop Morkie: part Maltese and part Yorkie. Lizzie tried to pay lots of attention to each of them, but she was distracted. She could not stop thinking about Bubbles.

On her way home, she walked up the Mooneys' brick pathway and knocked on their door. Nobody answered, but Lizzie could hear a baby crying inside. Shrieking, actually. That little Aria sure could make some noise!

Lizzie knocked louder and waited.

"Lizzie!" Mrs. Mooney answered the door with a screaming, red-faced Aria strapped to her front. "Didn't you get my message?" She bounced up and down, trying to quiet the wailing baby.

"I did," said Lizzie. "I know you didn't want me to walk Bubbles today. I just thought I would come by to make sure everything is okay." Lizzie thought Mrs. Mooney looked tired. No wonder, if the baby cried like that all the time.

Mrs. Mooney sighed. She bounced the baby some more. Aria's cries died down to sniffles.

"Come on in," said Mrs. Mooney. She led Lizzie into her living room and shoved aside some of the laundry that was piled on the couch. "I can't seem to get around to folding this lately," she said with an embarrassed smile.

"No problem," said Lizzie. "Where's Bubbles? Is she all right? I was beginning to worry about her."

"She's fine," said Mrs. Mooney. "She's probably upstairs, snoozing on her bed. That's where she spends a lot of time lately. She isn't sick — we've had the vet check her out — but she just doesn't seem to be herself lately. All she does is mope around. That's why I keep canceling. She doesn't even seem to care about going for walks anymore."

Lizzie nodded. "I noticed that." She paused. "Do you think it might have to do with . . . um . . ." She looked at the baby strapped to Mrs. Mooney's chest.

"Aria?" Mrs. Mooney asked. "Absolutely. My husband and I love Bubbles. She used to be the center of our universe. But now that Aria's here, we just don't have time to play with a dog. I know Bubbles misses our fun times, and I feel terrible about it, but what can you do? Babies need a lot of attention."

"So do puppies." Lizzie couldn't help herself; it just popped out.

Mrs. Mooney looked down. "I know. That's why I've been thinking we might need your help. Maybe it's time to find our sweet Bubbles a new home."

CHAPTER TWO

"Really?" Lizzie stared at Mrs. Mooney. Could this be the same person who had practically bought out the puppy toy section when she and her husband had first brought Bubbles home? The woman who had bought Bubbles a cushy bed fit for a princess? The one who fed her puppy nothing but the fanciest organic dog food?

Mrs. Mooney's eyes filled with tears. "Really," she said, "I will miss her with all my heart, but it's just not fair to Bubbles. We can't give her the attention she needs and deserves. I had no idea how much time and energy one little baby could take up." She kissed the top of Aria's head. The baby was asleep now, snoring softly through her adorable little nose.

Lizzie heard footsteps on the stairs, and then Bubbles appeared in the living room. She was so cute, with her springy brown curls. She stretched her front paws forward and lifted her nose high. Then she shook herself all over and yawned, showing her pretty little pink tongue.

Did I hear my name?

"Bubbles!" Lizzie said. "Come here, girl." She patted her knee encouragingly. "Come say hi."

Bubbles ambled over, taking her time. She let Lizzie scratch her between the ears, but Lizzie noticed that the puppy's eyes were on Mrs. Mooney. Mrs. Mooney didn't seem to notice. She was looking down at Aria and smoothing her baby's hair while she hummed a soft tune under her breath.

Lizzie couldn't help thinking that Bubbles looked sad as she gazed at her owner.

What about me? Don't you want to pet me anymore?

"It wouldn't be hard at all to find Bubbles a great home," Lizzie said. "She's so pretty and smart." She was just thinking out loud, but Mrs. Mooney nodded and smiled.

"So you'll take her?" she asked. "I know your family fosters puppies. I've been trying to get up the nerve to ask you to help us. My husband and I just want Bubbles to be happy."

Lizzie gulped. "Are you sure?" she asked.

Mrs. Mooney nodded. "We've been talking it over and we really think it's the right thing to do."

"I have to check with my parents, so —" Lizzie began.

"Of course, of course," Mrs. Mooney said, interrupting her. "I know it's not something to rush into."

"So can I use your phone?" Lizzie finished.

Mrs. Mooney raised her eyebrows. "Oh! Right now?"

"Sure," said Lizzie. "Lots of times when our family fosters puppies we make a pretty quick decision. Especially when the puppy is as easy to take care of as Bubbles would be."

Mrs. Mooney reached into her jeans pocket and pulled out a phone. "Okay," she said. "I can't believe this is really happening."

But it did happen. Lizzie called home and talked to her mom. Mom said it was okay with her but told Lizzie to check with Dad, so Lizzie called him at the fire station where he worked. "Sure," he said after Lizzie had explained about

Bubbles. "We've got room right now, and she sounds like a great dog to have around."

Mrs. Mooney cried a little and hugged Bubbles tight, but she agreed that it might be best if Bubbles was already gone by the time her husband returned from work. When Lizzie finally headed home, she had Bubbles on her leash next to her, and her backpack was stuffed with the puppy's favorite toys and treats.

Bubbles walked slowly, lagging behind Lizzie. When they got to the end of the block, she turned around as if it were time to go back home. She whimpered a little when Lizzie tugged on her leash.

"Aww," said Lizzie. "I know you'll miss your people, but we'll take care of you, I promise."

"Hey, Lizzie!" Maria waved from across the street. "Aren't you finished for the day yet?"

Maria Santiago was Lizzie's best friend and a partner in their dog-walking business. She loved dogs almost as much as Lizzie did.

Lizzie waited with Bubbles while Maria crossed the street to join them. "I'm done," she said. "But guess what? We're going to foster Bubbles."

"Really?" Maria knelt down to pet Bubbles's springy brown curls. "Why? She's, like, the cutest poodle in the world. She's mellow, too, not crazy like Pogo and Pixie." Those were a pair of poodles Maria often walked.

"Maybe a little too mellow lately," Lizzie said. "I guess Bubbles has been having a pretty hard time adjusting to having a baby in the house. She was used to a lot of attention, and now she's not number one anymore."

"Poor Bubbles," said Maria. "And now they're just giving her up?"

"Mrs. Mooney seems really upset about it," said

Lizzie, "but she wants to do what's right for Bubbles."

Maria nodded and stood up. "Well, I'm sure you'll find her a great home. And she'll probably cheer up once she's at your house, with Buddy and all."

Lizzie said good-bye to her friend and headed off with Bubbles. "Maria's right," Lizzie said to the puppy. "Buddy will cheer you up. He always makes me feel better when I'm sad."

CHAPTER THREE

Lizzie walked up the driveway and tapped on the kitchen door. "We're here," she called to her mom. "Can you let Buddy out?" The Petersons usually had Buddy meet a new foster puppy in their fenced backyard. That way, the dogs had plenty of space and could take their time getting to know each other.

"I think you'll like it here," she told Bubbles as she opened the gate in the fence. She bent to unclip the leash from Bubbles's collar and ruffled the puppy's soft ears. "There! Now you can run around as much as you like."

Most of the Petersons' foster puppies dashed around the entire yard when they first arrived, sniffing everything and stopping to pee now and then as they learned about their new, temporary home. But Bubbles didn't run. She didn't even trot. She plodded to the stairs that went up to the deck, and sat near the bottom, her fluffy ears drooping.

Lizzie frowned. Bubbles was definitely not acting like herself. She wasn't acting like any other puppy Lizzie had known, either. "What's the matter, Bubbles?" Lizzie asked. She heard the sliding door open, and Buddy trotted out, ears up and an eager little doggy grin on his face. Lizzie couldn't help grinning back. Buddy was always happy to see her, and it made her feel great.

"Hey, Bud-man," she said. "Look! We have company."

Buddy had already figured that out. He rushed right down the steps to greet Bubbles. He wagged his tail hard as he sniffed and snuffled his happiest doggy hello. Then he jumped up to get his foam football and brought it back to show Bubbles. He stretched out his front paws and stuck his butt in the air, inviting her to play. Buddy loved nothing better than a merry game of chase around the yard.

Bubbles did not wag her tail. She didn't sniff Buddy back. She didn't seem the least bit interested in him or his toy. Lizzie watched carefully, ready to jump in if Bubbles growled or showed her teeth, but she didn't do that, either. Really, she just seemed bored. She yawned and lay down, chin on her paws.

Yes, okay, hello. I get it. You want to be friends. Whatever.

Buddy looked at Lizzie, as if asking her advice. Lizzie shrugged. "I guess she doesn't want to play right now," she said. Lizzie picked up the football and tossed it for him, and Buddy tore after it.

Bubbles just lay there.

Lizzie threw the ball a few more times for Buddy, hoping Bubbles would decide that fetch looked like a fun game after all, but the pretty brown pup never budged.

Bubbles didn't even look up when the sliding door opened again and Charles clattered down the stairs. "A new puppy?" he asked. "She's so cute!" He reached out to pet her, but Bubbles pulled back.

Lizzie saw the hurt look on Charles's face. Dogs usually warmed right up to Charles, and he was great with the puppies they fostered. "I think she's feeling kind of shy," Lizzie said. "Bubbles has had some pretty big changes in her life, and now she's here at a new place. We just have to give her some time — and space."

Charles nodded. He moved away and perched on a higher step. "That's cool," he said. "What does she like to do?"

"She used to love going for walks," Lizzie said. "And she always liked playing with certain toys, too, like . . ." She reached into her back-pack and pulled out the stuffed shark Mrs. Mooney had sent along. It was red, with huge white teeth, and it squeaked when Lizzie squeezed it. "Sharkie?" she asked Bubbles, showing her the toy.

Bubbles looked at the shark, but she didn't even sniff it. Lizzie sighed and put the toy down between the puppy's feet. "I don't know," she told Charles. "She just seems . . . sad."

"Maybe the Bean will cheer her up," Charles said. "Puppies always like the Bean." He stood up. "I'll go get him. He just got home from day care."

Lizzie did not have high hopes. Sure enough, when Charles came back out with their little brother, Bubbles didn't even seem to notice the new person. The Bean toddled over to her and held out his hand for her to sniff, the way he'd been taught to do with new dogs, but Bubbles didn't sniff. The Bean looked up at Lizzie. "Uppy sad?" he asked.

Lizzie nodded. "The puppy is sad," she said. Even the Bean could see it. The question was, what could they do about it? Bubbles didn't want to play with Buddy or with her toys. She didn't want to go for walks. And, Lizzie found out later that night, she didn't even seem very interested in her food.

"Maybe we should take her to the vet," Lizzie suggested after dinner. "Maybe there's really something wrong with her."

"Let's give her a couple of days to get used to us and our house," Dad suggested. "In the meantime, how about calling your aunt? She might have some ideas."

"Aunt Amanda!" Lizzie said. Of course. Her aunt knew everything about dogs. She ran a doggy day care called Bowser's Backyard and also had four dogs of her own. Lizzie went right to the phone.

By the time she went to bed that night, Lizzie felt a lot better. Aunt Amanda had promised to come over and meet Bubbles the very next afternoon, once she got her Saturday chores done at Bowser's. "She'll help us figure out how to help you," Lizzie told Bubbles. The puppy lay at the foot of her bed, curled into a tight little ball. Lizzie petted her soft, springy curls until the sweet brown pup relaxed into sleep. Then she pulled up her covers and went to sleep, too, hoping that Bubbles would soon be her old bubbly self.

CHAPTER FOUR

"I give up," Lizzie said when Aunt Amanda arrived the next afternoon. "I've tried everything I can think of, and I just can't make Bubbles happy." Lizzie had spent her whole Saturday morning trying to cheer Bubbles up, but nothing had worked. When the doorbell rang, Lizzie had been sitting slumped on the couch, feeling as sad as Bubbles seemed to feel. Aunt Amanda patted her shoulder. "Don't worry," she said. "We'll figure this out. Tell me what you've tried." She knelt down and called softly to Bubbles. "Come on, darling. Come say hi. I don't bite, I promise."

Bubbles lay on the living room rug, her chin

propped on Sharkie. She cocked an eyebrow at Aunt Amanda but didn't move.

"See?" Lizzie said. "That's all she does all day. We tried playing Find the Biscuit, but she just ended up coming in here and lying down again, every time."

Find the Biscuit was Buddy's favorite game. Lizzie would take him into the kitchen and make him sit and stay. She always showed him the biscuit so he knew what he was going to be looking for. He would sniff it, then look up at her eagerly. His wagging tail would thump the floor the whole time Lizzie was in the living room, tucking the biscuit under a couch cushion or stashing it in between some magazines on the coffee table. When Lizzie came back into the kitchen and said, "Okay, Buddy — find it!" he would jump up and race into the living room, tail wagging faster and faster as he sniffed and snuffled until he found the treat. No sooner had he crunched it down than he would race back into the kitchen, begging for another round.

That morning, Buddy had been happy to demonstrate the whole Find the Biscuit routine for Bubbles. He did it three times before Dad and the Bean took him off to the park so Lizzie could work with the new puppy. Each of those times, Bubbles had followed Buddy into the living room, but that had been about it. Once she was there, Bubbles would settle into a spot between the couch and Dad's armchair where she seemed to feel safe. She would lie there, resting her chin on Sharkie and watching Buddy hunt for buried treasure.

Lizzie explained all this to her aunt. "After Dad left with Buddy, I tried hiding a biscuit again, and she did the same thing," she said. "I thought maybe she didn't want to compete with Buddy for the biscuit — but no, she just wasn't really interested in the biscuit."

"Have you tried tastier treats to get her excited?" Aunt Amanda asked. "Like" — she dug in her pocket, frowning, then pulled out a stick of string cheese — "this?" She peeled the wrapper, broke off a piece, and held it out to Bubbles. "Do you like cheese, honey?"

Lizzie saw Bubbles's nose twitching as she sniffed from across the room. For a moment her eyes brightened, but then she yawned and lay down.

What's the big deal about cheese, anyway?

"Hmmm," said Aunt Amanda. "What else have you tried?"

Lizzie held up her hand and ticked off fingers. "Which Hand Is the Treat In, Hide-and-Seek,

Tug with Sharkie . . ." She paused. "Let's see. I guess that's it. Plus last night we worked on her basic obedience — she's pretty good at sit and stay and lie down — and I tried to teach her how to sit up pretty."

"That's a lot," said Aunt Amanda. "It may be the most attention she's had in a while, since the baby arrived at the Mooneys'." She stroked her chin. "I wonder if she's overwhelmed."

Lizzie shook her head. "She doesn't act stressed out. I know what that looks like. She's not pacing around panting, or drooling, or whining. She just seems bored, and sad." She nodded toward Bubbles. "I mean, look at her."

Bubbles had fallen asleep with her chin on Sharkie. Her nose twitched and her paws moved for a second, as if she was dreaming about chasing squirrels, but then she heaved a sigh and was still again.

Aunt Amanda shook her head. "Poor thing. Well, many people believe that dogs can get depressed, just like people can. For dogs it happens sometimes if another pet in the family dies, or when people split up or move. Or . . . when there's a new baby in the picture. It's not really that unusual."

"Will she be sad forever?" Lizzie asked. "I mean, how are we going to find her a new home when she's like this? Nobody wants a dog who just mopes around all the time. She doesn't even want to eat."

"Moping and a lack of appetite are definitely signs of depression," said Aunt Amanda. "But no, it won't last forever. Bubbles just needs attention, and time. If we're patient, I'm sure she'll bounce back."

"I've given her lots of attention," said Mom, who had just come into the room. "Mostly she ignores me. Sometimes she goes to the door and scratches as if she needs to go out, but when I take her out, she doesn't have to pee. She just tries to pull me down the street toward the Mooneys'."

"Sure. She wants to go home," said Aunt Amanda. "But home isn't the same anymore, and she wouldn't be happy there, either. I think all the things you're doing are great, and you should keep doing them. Attention, games, treats . . . If she doesn't cheer up soon, you might want to take her to the vet for another checkup, just to make sure nothing else is wrong. The vet might even talk to you about giving Bubbles medication to make her feel better."

"Wow," said Lizzie. She went over and lay down next to Bubbles on the rug. "We'll be patient with you," she told the puppy as she stroked the silky-soft fur on Bubbles's ears. "I sure hope you'll feel happier soon."

The front door opened and Charles walked in,

home from a sleepover at his new friend Manuel's. "Hi, sweetie," said Mom.

"Hi," said Charles. He had his arms crossed in front of his chest, and he moved quickly toward the stairs.

"What have you got there?" Mom asked.

"Nothing," said Charles.

Then Manuel and his dad appeared at the door. Manuel's dad was holding a large wire cage. "Where do you want to put the cage?" he asked.

"Cage?" Mom asked.

"For Boo," said Manuel.

"Who's Boo?" Mom looked confused.

Charles sighed and opened his arms just enough so they could all see what he was holding. A small white bunny stared back at them without blinking. He wrinkled his nose and twitched his ears. "This is Boo," said Charles. "I said we could keep him for a while."

CHAPTER FIVE

"A — a bunny?" Mom asked. "Charles Peterson, what were you thinking?" She glared at him, then turned to Manuel's father. "I think there must be some mistake here," she said, smiling.

Lizzie jumped up. "A bunny?" she asked. She had always liked bunnies, and often wondered whether it would be fun to have one for a pet. Supposedly, they could be just as friendly and trainable as dogs. Bubbles jumped up, too, and followed Lizzie to Charles's side. Bubbles stretched out her neck, trying to sniff the bunny.

"No, Bubbles!" said Lizzie, shooing her away. "Great. That's the first interest she's shown in anything, and it's only because she wants to chase it." She knew that dogs loved to chase bunnies in the woods.

"You'd better keep them separated," said Aunt Amanda, who had also come over to see the bunny.

"You bet we'll keep them separated," Mom said, crossing her arms. "Like, in different houses." She smiled at Manuel's dad again. "I'm so sorry, but we can't possibly —"

"But neither can we!" he said. "We're going away for the rest of the weekend. I don't know what Manuel was thinking."

"Boo is the classroom pet in Manuel's room," said Charles. "But nobody in his class is really that into bunnies. Nobody ever plays with him or wants to take him home on weekends. Right, Manuel?"

Manuel nodded. "Our teacher Ms. Wellborne said it's probably time to find Boo a new place to live, where he'll be happier. I felt sorry for him," he said. "That's why I took him home for the weekend. But really he's kind of boring. All he does is eat and sleep." He held up a bag of bunny pellets to show what the bunny ate.

"He's a good guy," said Manuel's dad. "He doesn't bite or kick, like I hear some rabbits do." He smiled hopefully at Mom.

Charles looked down at the small soft bundle in his arms. "Boo is a foster bunny," he said. "Just like all the puppies we take care of. He needs a new home, where people appreciate him. Please, can't we keep him, at least for the rest of the weekend? His cage can be in my room, and I promise I'll take care of him and keep him safe." He looked up at Mom, and Lizzie thought her brother looked almost as irresistible as Buddy did when Buddy was begging for a treat. Charles's eyes shone, and he had a pleading look. "Please? Boo needs us."

Bubbles was still trying to sniff Boo. Lizzie pulled the puppy away with one hand while she reached out to stroke the bunny's ears with the other. "Oh, he's so soft!" she said. Boo gazed up at her with wide eyes as he wrinkled his nose and twitched his ears, and Lizzie felt her heart flip over. It was like love at first sight: bunny love. He was so adorable! "Mom, please?" she said, putting on her own best begging face. "We'll find out all about bunnies and learn how to take care of him. It's practically like a project for school. It'll be educational!"

Manuel and his dad stood there silently.

Mom turned to Aunt Amanda with a pleading look. "What about you? Could you take him?" she asked.

Aunt Amanda shook her head. "No way," she said. "My house is already overrun with animals."

Mom threw up her hands. "Oh, fine," she said. "I can see there's no way out. But that rabbit stays in his cage! I do not want bunny poop all over my house."

Bunny poop. Lizzie felt a giggle bubble up, but she managed to hold it in. "Thanks, Mom!" she said.

"Yeah, thanks!" said Charles. He gestured up the stairs. "My room's up there," he told Manuel's dad.

As he followed the man with the cage up the stairs, Charles turned and screwed up his face at Lizzie. She knew he was trying to wink — he still hadn't quite figured out how to shut one eye at a time — so she winked back. They had won the battle! Mom had not been able to resist their expert begging.

Bubbles watched Charles go up the stairs. She pranced away from Lizzie and put one dainty paw on the bottom step.

Wait! I wanted to get to know you. I think we could be friends.

"Man, she really wants that bunny," said Lizzie as she grabbed the puppy's collar. "Don't worry," she told Mom. "It'll be okay."

Mom nodded tiredly. "Right," she said. She shook her head. "How did I even get into this?" she added, as if to herself. "I used to be a cat person, and now it's puppies and bunnies, twenty-four seven. What's next, a boa constrictor?"

Lizzie laughed. "No worries, Mom," she said. "I'd have one, but you know how Charles feels about snakes. Dad's scared of them, too!"

She led Bubbles back to the living room and tried again to interest her in a game of tug with Sharkie, but Bubbles just rested her chin on her paws and gazed at the stairs, where the bunny had last been seen. "Oh, Bubbles," said Lizzie. "When will you ever cheer up?"

Aunt Amanda knelt down and stroked Bubbles's soft fur. "I know it's frustrating," she said. "But just try to be patient. She needs some time. If you give her enough attention and try to keep her busy, I'm sure she'll bounce back to her old self."

Manuel and his dad came back down the stairs. "Thanks, 'bye!" they called as they let themselves out. It was obvious that they were relieved to get rid of the bunny.

"'Bye," called Mom. Then she sighed. "Well," she said, turning to Aunt Amanda and Lizzie, "I guess we're a puppy *and* bunny foster family now. I don't even know what they eat besides those pellets. Do they like carrots? Or is that just Bugs Bunny?"

"I'll find out!" Lizzie jumped to her feet. "I'll go to the library. Remember I promised I would learn about bunnies? I have books to return anyway. I'll see if they have a book about bunnies."

Aunt Amanda nodded. "Good idea. I'll drop you at the library on my way home," she said.

"Thanks! Maybe they have some new dog books, too," said Lizzie as she ran for her jacket. "Maybe I can find some more ideas on how to help Bubbles."

CHAPTER SIX

"Oh, look! Two of my favorite people." Sandy beamed at Lizzie and Charles. "Two people who look like they're on a mission." She came around her desk. "How can I help you?" Sandy, a children's librarian at the Littleton Library, was always happy when people came in with questions — and she always seemed to be able to help find the answers.

"Do you have any books about iguanas?" Charles asked. He had decided to go with Lizzie to the library because he had a science report to do over the weekend. Mom had promised to watch

Bubbles and Boo and keep them separate while Lizzie and Charles were gone.

"Of course," said Sandy. That was what Sandy always said. She started toward the shelves — Sandy never needed to check the computer to know where things were — but Lizzie stopped her.

"Wait!" Lizzie said, frowning at Charles. "We're really here to learn about rabbits. Like bunnies. The kind people keep as pets."

"No problem," Sandy said cheerfully. "They're in the same general area. Follow me." She led them toward the nonfiction shelves, then paused, thinking for a second as she ran a finger over a row of books. "Right . . . here," she said, pulling one out. "'The Family Rabbit,'" she said, reading the cover. "Does that sound good? I know we have one other rabbit book that's very popular, but it looks like it's out right now."

"This will be a great start," Lizzie said. "Thanks!" She headed for the reading nook while Sandy helped Charles look for iguana books.

The reading nook was a comfortable place, filled with big soft pillows and plenty of places to curl up with a book. There was a small stage nearby, where Sandy sometimes sat to play guitar and sing silly songs for toddlers and their parents. Lizzie loved to go along when Mom took the Bean. On those days the reading nook was filled with crawling kids banging on tambourines or humming through buzzy kazoos. Today it was quiet and peaceful.

Lizzie planned to check out the book Sandy had given her, but she couldn't wait to get home to start learning about bunnies. She opened *The Family Rabbit* and began to flip through it. By the time Charles joined her, she had already learned what kind of bunny Boo was. "Look," she said, showing him a picture. "I think Boo might be a Florida rabbit, even though his eyes are brown instead of red. Florida rabbits are usually white, and he's the right shape and size, I think. It says that they're great with kids, too."

"What else does it say about bunnies?" Charles asked.

"A lot," said Lizzie. She flipped through the pages. "Like they do eat carrots, but what they need most is fresh greens — lots of them — and plenty of water. And pellet food, too. And guess what else they need? Exercise. Bunnies aren't supposed to be in their cages all day long, any more than you'd leave a dog in a crate. They're supposed to get out and have playtime for at least a couple of hours a day."

"Interesting," said Charles. "Maybe one reason everybody in Manuel's class thinks Boo is boring is because he's bored! But what about the . . . you know, the pooping problem?" he asked. "I mean, if he's running around in the house?"

"First of all, you can train them to use a litter box, just like cats," Lizzie said, quickly scanning a chapter on basic rabbit care. "And second, it's better if they're maybe just in one room, not *all* over the house, because they can be destructive. It says here that they love to chew on electric wires and cables. Also, he doesn't have to get exercise only in the house. He can be outside, as long as we have a safe space. He'd probably love our backyard."

"I bet he would," said Charles. "I hope we get to keep Boo for a while, at least until we find him the right home."

Lizzie nodded. "Plus, look what it says here," she said, pointing to the caption under a picture of two bunnies. "Rabbits like company. They can get lonely on their own, so it's not such a great idea to have only one bunny."

Charles snorted. "Right. You think Mom's going to let us get another bunny just to keep Boo company?"

Lizzie smiled. "Maybe not. At least not right away. But maybe she'll learn to love having a bunny around. Boo is pretty cute."

They took their books up to the desk to check them out. "All set?" Sandy asked. "I'll let you know when that other bunny book is returned. Sounds like you two might be getting a new pet. Will it be a bunny or an iguana, though? That's the question."

Lizzie laughed. "No iguanas for now. We're fostering a bunny, though. And also a really cute poodle puppy named Bubbles."

"Wow!" said Sandy. "Maybe they'd both like to be in our pet show." She pushed a flyer across the desk. "It's going to be a lot of fun. Costumes, contests, games . . . I can't wait to see the library lawn full of pets!"

"Cool," said Lizzie, looking at the flyer. "Great idea."

"I figured a pet show would be a fun way to be around a lot of animals," Sandy said. "My boyfriend isn't really an animal person, so I don't have any pets of my own right now, but I love animals — all kinds. Well, maybe I'm not that crazy about iguanas," she told Charles with a wink. "They're not so cuddly."

"You can come visit Bubbles and Boo anytime," said Lizzie. "It's good for our foster animals to meet lots of different people."

"And I'll show you my report when it's finished," Charles told her. "Maybe you'll change your mind when you find out how cool iguanas are."

Lizzie and Charles headed home, arguing about

which of them should get to take Boo to the pet show. They both knew that an adorable white bunny was sure to win some prizes. "I'm the one who brought him home," said Charles.

"But I'm the one who's going to learn all about how to take care of him," said Lizzie as she pushed open the back door.

"But his cage is going to be in my room —" Charles was saying when Mom appeared in the doorway between the kitchen and the living room.

"Shhh," she said, her finger over her lips. "Follow me. Quietly. You're not going to believe this."

CHAPTER SEVEN

Lizzie peeked around the doorway into the living room. "You're kidding me!" she said. She put her hand over her mouth. "That is the most adorable thing I ever saw in my whole life."

"What?" Charles poked his head around, too. "Wow!" he said. "Look at them!"

Bubbles and Boo lay together on the rug, fast asleep. The white bunny was spooned cozily into the curve of the soft brown puppy's belly. Boo's long ears twitched gently, and Lizzie could hear him making a soft hiccuping noise. Somehow, she knew it meant that Boo was very, very happy.

Lizzie whirled around to look at her mother. Mom was smiling the way she did when she was holding someone's tiny baby. "I know," Mom said softly. "And you didn't even see the best part, when they were playing together."

"Playing?" Lizzie stared at her mother.

"Like they'd been best friends forever," her mom said. "Chasing each other around the room, jumping, wrestling . . ." She shook her head. "It was amazing. They wore themselves out."

"Speaking of 'out,'" said Charles as all three of them stepped back into the kitchen so they wouldn't wake the sleepers, "how did Boo get out of his cage, anyway? I thought we were going to keep them apart."

Mom picked an orange out of the bowl on the counter and rolled it around in her hands. "Well," she said, and Lizzie noticed that she was blushing, "that was my fault. After you left, I went up to your room to make sure everything was okay. Boo was so cute that I couldn't resist letting him out of his cage for a little cuddle. I was sure I latched it when I put him back in, but . . ." She shrugged. "I guess I wasn't so careful about closing the door to your room, either."

"Moommmmm," Lizzie and Charles chorused together. "Baaad Moommm!"

She hung her head. "I know," she said. "We're going to have to be very careful about that latch."

"So then what happened?" Lizzie asked.

Mom laughed. "I was upstairs in my office, and suddenly I heard this crazy ruckus downstairs. I ran down and caught them racing around. At first I was terrified — I thought Bubbles was trying to catch Boo — but the next minute Boo was jumping over Bubbles, just for fun! It was hilarious. They both seemed so happy that I just

let them run and play until they tired themselves out."

Lizzie sat down at the kitchen table and paged
through her rabbit book. "Yes!" she said. "It says
right here that rabbits can get along with all sorts
of other pets. They love having friends. This is so
great for Bubbles! Now we have to keep Boo for a
while."

"Yeah!" said Charles. "I'm sure they don't want
him back in Manuel's classroom. Let's keep him
forever!"

Mom held up her hands. "Hold on, hold on. Let's
take it one day at a time."

"Hey, what's that thumping noise?" Lizzie
asked. She jumped up and ran into the living
room. Boo and Bubbles had woken up, and now
they were racing around the couch at top speed.
Bubbles chased Boo, and Boo leapt over Bubbles,
up over the back of the couch. Bubbles scrambled

around the couch to catch the bunny, but Boo zoomed off, leaping onto Dad's chair. The poodle's ears bounced gaily as she pranced, and her tail did not stop wagging for a second. The rabbit hopped off the chair and up onto the couch again, then leapt over the puppy while Bubbles lay on her back, legs waving happily in the air.

Lizzie was laughing so hard she could hardly breathe. "Did you see that? Boo did a binky!" she said to Charles and Mom, who were also watching and laughing. "I can't believe it. I just read about that in the book."

"What's a binky?" Charles asked.

"Watch, I bet he'll do it again. When rabbits get really, really happy, they race around, then jump in the air and twist their bodies and flick their feet. People call that move a binky."

"There he goes!" Charles pointed and laughed as Boo leapt into the air, kicking out his feet so he landed in a whole different direction. Then the rabbit raced off again, leaping and twisting, and Bubbles raced after him, barking excitedly.

"Okay, okay," Mom said. "Maybe it's time to take this show outside. They're getting a little too rambunctious for this room."

Lizzie knelt down and called Bubbles to her. She hugged Bubbles tight and felt tears come into her eyes. "I'm so happy you're feeling better again," she whispered as she petted the puppy's soft curls.

Meanwhile, Charles waited until Boo stopped running. Then he picked the rabbit up carefully, cradling his back legs, the same way he would pick up a young puppy. Lizzie led the way to the sliding door that opened to the deck and backyard.

Boo was so excited to be outdoors that he raced around the entire yard three times, leaping over bushes and darting under patio furniture, before he settled down to nibble on some grass. Bubbles ran around, too, then found Sharkie on the lawn and brought the toy to Lizzie. Bubbles's eyes shone and her tail wagged as she went into a play bow, her front legs stretched way out and her butt in the air. She chomped hard on the shark to make it squeak, shook the toy, and chomped it again.

Want to play? I can teach you how to play fetch if you want. I'm really good at it! Wait and see!

Lizzie laughed as she took Sharkie and threw the toy across the yard. It was great to see Bubbles happy again. Lizzie turned around when she heard someone coming onto the deck. "Mom!" she began, but then she stopped. It wasn't Mom. It was Sandy, the librarian.

Sandy waved. "Hi," she said. "Bet you didn't think you'd see me this soon." She held up a book. "This bunny-care book was returned just after you left, so I thought I'd drop it off on my way home from work. Besides, you said I could come meet your foster pets, and I just couldn't wait." She sat down next to Lizzie on the deck steps. "Wow, look at them! They get along great, don't they?" She held out her hands, and Bubbles pranced over to say hello. Sandy rubbed the puppy's ears.

Lizzie nodded. "You should have seen Bubbles before. She was not a happy dog, but now she is. I think being around Boo really cheered her up."

Charles picked up Boo and brought him to meet Sandy. "Awww! This guy would cheer anybody up," the librarian said as she stroked Boo's long ears. Lizzie could tell that Sandy really did love animals — all kinds.

"Maybe you can convince your boyfriend to have a bunny," said Lizzie.

"I wish," Sandy said. She did not seem very hopeful. "But I'm sure you'll find this cutie a good home soon." She kissed Boo's nose.

"I hope so," said Lizzie. "And as for Bubbles, I think I know just the home for her."

Bubbles was back to being the puppy Lizzie used to know — the playful, friendly, energetic pooch the Mooneys had once showered with attention and love. If only they could see her now! Maybe the best forever family for Bubbles was the Mooneys after all. Lizzie just knew that Mrs. Mooney would be glad to have the puppy back, now that Bubbles was happy again.

CHAPTER EIGHT

Lizzie couldn't wait for the Mooneys to see that Bubbles was back to her old self. She knew they would be thrilled. First thing on Sunday morning, she took Bubbles for a walk. The puppy pranced along in front of Lizzie, eagerly making her way up the sidewalk. She sniffed at every bush and every mailbox. She even stuck her nose straight up in the air and sniffed, tossing her fluffy ears back as she took deep breaths.

Ah, what a beautiful morning! So many delicious smells to smell.

Lizzie marched up the walk to the Mooneys' house and knocked on the door. This time, Mr. Mooney answered. "Oh! Hello, Lizzie. Nice to see you. And . . . you brought Bubbles." He looked bewildered, but when Bubbles rushed at him and wriggled happily, he smiled and scratched her between the ears. "Hi, princess," he murmured to her. "Hi, there, darling girl."

Lizzie heard crying in the background. So did Mr. Mooney. He stood up and glanced toward the living room. "Sounds like Aria needs some attention. Um, it was nice of you to bring Bubbles by for a visit, but right now we —"

"I brought her back because she's happy again," said Lizzie. "You can see it, right? She's over her sadness. I think she'd really, really like to be back home with you."

Mr. Mooney stared at Lizzie. "Aw, gee, I don't know," he said. "We already talked and talked about this, my wife and I. It was a really hard decision, but we're sure it was the right one."

Lizzie thought he didn't sound very sure. And she noticed the loving way he gazed down at Bubbles. "Please?" she asked. "Just take her for today and see what you think."

"Martin?" Mrs. Mooney's voice came from inside, rising over Aria's cries. "Who's at the door? We need your help in here."

Lizzie gave Bubbles a quick kiss good-bye. "Be good," she whispered. She headed back down the walk before Mr. Mooney could say anything else. She kept her fingers crossed the whole way home. If only the Mooneys would keep Bubbles after all.

When she arrived home, she found Charles sitting on the couch in the living room with Boo on his lap. Charles was reading *The Family Rabbit* as he stroked Boo's ears. Lizzie sat down beside him and reached over to pet Boo's soft nose. "Did you read about how you can teach bunnies to go over little jumps?" she asked. "They're very trainable."

"It says here that we need to get him some toys, too," said Charles. "Or make him some. I guess rabbits love things they can hide in, like shoe boxes."

"Has he done any binkies lately?" Lizzie asked. She wanted to see Boo run and twist and jump again. "His binkies are so hilarious."

Charles shook his head. "He's been pretty quiet ever since you left. I tried to tempt him with some lettuce, but he didn't seem interested."

"Boo is probably tired after all that playing yesterday," Lizzie said. "I hope that's all it is, anyway. He'd better not get sick before the pet show next week." She stroked Boo's soft fur. "You're going to be the cutest pet there," she told him.

"Right," said Charles. "And I've been taking really good care of him. That's why I get to be the one to bring him to the pet show."

Lizzie glared at him. "But I have a great costume idea," she said. She didn't really, but she knew she had plenty of time to think of one.

"So do I!" said Charles. "But I'm not telling you, 'cause you'll steal it."

"You do not have an idea," said Lizzie. "You're just saying that." She reached into Charles's lap to take Boo, but Charles held the bunny tightly.

"He's mine!" Charles said.

"Is not!" said Lizzie.

Mom appeared in the doorway. "I don't want to hear you two fighting," she said. "If you can't be nice to each other, we're not going to keep that rabbit. I don't know why I let you talk me into it in the first place."

"Okay, Mom," said Lizzie. "We'll be nice." Lizzie and Charles gave each other fake smiles. Mom turned to leave, and Lizzie scowled at Charles. "Give me the bunny," she whispered.

63

"No!" Charles cradled Boo in his arms. "He's mine."

"No, he's not, he's our whole family's foster bunny," said Lizzie. "Come on, let me hold him."

While Charles and Lizzie squabbled, Boo just lay there, snoozing sometimes or just sitting and watching them, his nose wrinkling and his ears laid back and twitching. He did not seem like the same bunny who had raced around the room the night before. He seemed — boring. Lizzie was even starting to think maybe she'd rather take Buddy to the pet show instead, even though he hated getting dressed up.

Then the doorbell rang.

Lizzie answered the door to see Mr. and Mrs. Mooney standing on the front steps. Mr. Mooney had Aria strapped to his chest, and Mrs. Mooney had Bubbles on a leash. "I'm sorry, but it's not working out," Mrs. Mooney said. "She's moping around again, and we just can't —"

Lizzie saw Bubbles's ears perk up. She saw the puppy's eyes brighten. The next thing she knew, Bubbles had bolted right past her, into the house. Two seconds later, Bubbles was chasing Boo around the living room, and both of them looked even happier than they had the night before.

Mr. and Mrs. Mooney watched, their mouths hanging open in surprise.

Lizzie just laughed. "I guess these two have to be a package deal from now on," she said to them. "What would you think about adopting a bunny?"

The Mooneys were back in their car and halfway down the block before Lizzie could even say good-bye.

CHAPTER NINE

"Look! There's another Princess Leia!" said Lizzie, pointing. "A pug this time. That's so funny. I have to get a picture of her and the Weimaraner Princess Leia together."

One week after the Mooneys had fled, Lizzie and Charles were at the library pet show. They strolled around the library lawn, Lizzie holding Bubbles on a leash and Charles holding Boo in his arms. Boo had a harness on, and Charles had a leash in his pocket, in case the bunny decided to get frisky.

So far, both animals were just taking in the whole scene, the same way Charles and Lizzie were. Bubbles's ears were perked up, and her eyes shone as she looked here and there, sniffing constantly. Boo's ears were also up, and he wrinkled his little nose and snuggled into Charles's chest as he stared with big eyes at the wild party around him.

Lizzie thought the little rabbit must be even more overwhelmed than she was, surrounded by so many animals — many of them in crazy costumes. Plenty of people and pets had turned out for the event. There was a black Lab dressed like a reindeer, a cat in a pirate outfit, three dachshunds all dressed like hot dogs with swirls of mustard up their backs, and a Great Dane who came as a bucking bronco, wearing a saddle with a stuffed cowboy on it. Lizzie saw princesses in all shapes and sizes, and a bulldog dressed as Batman, and a tiny Chihuahua whose costume made him look as if he were being eaten by a shark. She waved and smiled at the pet own-ers she knew: Jerry Small from the bookstore; Charles's best friend, Sammy, and his parents; and even Chief Olson from the firehouse were there.

"This is amazing," she said to Charles. "But I still think our costumes are best."

Charles gave her a high five. "And the sim-plest," he said.

Charles and Lizzie had stopped squabbling the night Bubbles came home — at least about which of them got to take Boo to the pet show. "Boo and Bubbles are obviously besties forever," Lizzie had said that night as they watched the animal friends snuggle together. "They can't be sepa-rated. We'll both take both of them."

As soon as they had agreed to that, they started arguing about something else: what costumes Bubbles and Boo would wear. "I think Bubbles would make a great Wookiee," Lizzie said. "And Boo could be an adorable Darth Vader."

"But those two characters are enemies," said Charles. "Bubbles and Boo are friends. They should dress up as famous friends. Like — like Frog and Toad."

Lizzie crossed her arms. It made her mad that Charles had come up with such a great idea. Why hadn't she thought of that? "No, how about Lilo and Stitch?" she asked. "Or Henry and Mudge? Or — hey, what about . . ."

Charles said it at the same moment Lizzie did. "Pooh and Piglet!"

It was so easy! All it took was an old red T-shirt of the Bean's that fitted Bubbles perfectly and a tiny pink-and-purple striped shirt for Boo. Lizzie made a "hunny pot" out of an empty oatmeal container and there they were: Winnie-the-Pooh and Piglet, the very best friends ever. Boo's striped shirt had come from Lizzie's Piglet stuffie, so it was even authentic.

Now, on the library lawn, Lizzie looked at the animal friends. She smiled. Bubbles's reddish-brown curls made her look just like the pudgy Pooh, and Boo's adorable long ears flopped just like Piglet's. Lizzie knew that Sandy, the librarian, would love costumes that were based on book characters. Bubbles and Boo were a sure bet to win the costume contest.

Bubbles wagged her tail hard as she gazed up at Lizzie.

This is so much fun! Why don't you let me off the leash so I can run around and play with all these friends!

"Welcome, everyone!" Sandy was standing at the top of the library stairs. She waved her arms for quiet. "I'm so glad to see you all here. I'm in animal heaven, to tell you the truth! We're about to start the parade, so you can start lining up near the door to the children's room. You'll march around the library three times, and the judges will be watching. After the parade, we'll announce the Best Costume winners, and then we'll start the other contests. Is everybody ready?"

A big cheer went up, and everyone milled around for a while, shaping themselves into some sort of parade. Then they began to march. Bubbles walked happily in front of Lizzie, her tail waving proudly. After their first lap around the library, Lizzie waved at Sandy, who was still standing on the stairs. Sandy came down and joined them in the parade. "Hi, Lizzie. Hi, Charles. Hi, Bubbles and Boo!" Bubbles put up a paw without even having to be told to shake. Sandy giggled as she took it. "Nice to see you again. Great costumes!"

she said to Lizzie. "Piglet and Pooh. So adorable. If I was one of the judges, I'd be voting for them." She scratched Bubbles between the ears and stroked Boo's ears. "I thought Bubbles was going back to her owners," she said. "Are you still fostering her? And what about Boo? Is he going back to his classroom?"

Lizzie shook her head. "Both of them definitely need new homes," she said. During the week Mom had checked with Manuel's teacher, who had said she was hoping to start over again with a different classroom pet — maybe an iguana!

"The only problem is that it turns out that these two come as a set," Lizzie went on. She told Sandy about how Bubbles and Boo were only happy when they were together. "Lots of people love dogs, and lots of people love bunnies — but not too many people love both or want to take on two new pets at once."

"Huh," said Sandy. "Well, I was hoping to talk to you about something — but right now I'd better run. The parade's almost over and then it'll be time for the contests. Such a busy day!"

Lizzie wondered what Sandy had wanted to talk to her about. Maybe she had an idea about a new home for Boo. It probably wouldn't work out anyway, now that Bubbles and Boo were a package deal.

During the parade's third lap around the library, Lizzie saw Maria arrive and waved her over to join her and Charles.

"Love the costumes!" Maria said as she petted Bubbles and Boo. "You'll win the contest for sure. Maybe you'll even get your picture in the paper, and someone will see it and want to adopt these two!"

"Attention, everyone!" Sandy's voice boomed over the microphone. "The judges have made their decisions and it's time to announce our contest winners."

One of the judges, a lady in a red "I ♥ Brittany spaniels" T-shirt, handed Sandy an envelope. Sandy opened it and began to read out loud the names of the winners. "In third place, we have Bitsy and Squiggles, as martians," she said. She paused while everybody applauded for the adorable Pomeranians in green alien costumes. "In second place, the judges chose Snookums the pirate." More applause, for the big orange tabby cat who'd won. "And in first place . . ."

Maria reached out for Lizzie's hand and squeezed it. "Good luck," she whispered.

"Maximus, the bucking bronco!" announced Sandy. The crowd went wild as the Great Dane trotted up for his prize, the stuffed cowboy on his back bobbing crazily like a broncobuster taking a ride.

Disappointed, Lizzie bit her lip as she clapped along with everyone else. Bubbles and Boo were the cutest pets at the show; she knew they were! Why couldn't the judges see that, too? She watched as the photographer from the *Littleton News* shot picture after picture of the winners. Maria was right. Winning the costume contest could have helped her find a new home for Bubbles and Boo. Had they missed their big chance?

CHAPTER TEN

"Sorry," Maria whispered.

Lizzie shrugged. "Those other costumes were pretty great," she said. "At least we still have a chance to win one of the other contests." With luck, the photographer would stick around for the rest of the day.

The girls walked on, with Charles behind them, holding Boo. Everyone who saw the bunny wanted to pet him, so Charles moved slowly through the crowd.

"Which contests did you sign up for?" asked Maria, scanning the oversized sign-up sheets that were posted on a big bulletin board.

"Best Tail-Wagger," Lizzie said. "Bubbles is a great tail-wagger now that she's happy again, aren't you, girl?" She smiled down at Bubbles, and Bubbles grinned back up at her, wiggling her whole back end.

Life is great, isn't it? Especially with good friends around.

"I also signed her up for the Whole Hog contest, but I have no idea how she'll do," Lizzie said. "That's the one where you try to get your dog to eat things like a lettuce leaf or an olive. If a dog refuses to eat anything, he's out. The winner is the one who eats everything the judge gives him."

"Buddy would have done great," said Charles. "He'll eat anything."

"What about Boo?" asked Maria. "I mean, Piglet."

Charles shrugged. "He doesn't do any tricks yet," he said, "but he can learn."

Just then, Sandy announced the tail-wagging contest. "Come on up, everyone," she said. She had the contestants line up and told them to do anything it took to get their dogs' tails wagging.

Lizzie waved to Charles. "Hey, get Boo where Bubbles can see him," she called.

"One, two, three, go!" said Sandy. The crowd roared with laughter as dog owners squeaked toys, made kissy noises, dangled hot dogs, and generally made fools of themselves as they tried to show off their dogs' tail-wagging skills. Lizzie just stood back and let Bubbles gaze at Boo. The puppy pulled at the leash, wagging her tail hard as she tried to get back to her friend.

C'mon! Boo's right there waiting for me! It's time for more play.

In the end, Bubbles didn't win that contest; a golden retriever with a huge plume of a tail got the most applause from the audience. Bubbles didn't win the Whole Hog contest, either. She ate a piece of apple and even a few bites of kale, but she turned up her nose at a pickle. The black Lab next to her gobbled everything his owner showed him, and walked away with the prize.

Sandy handed out medals to all the contest winners, then announced even more awards, like Best Ears, which went to a basset hound, and Cutest Bark, which went to a little black-and-white mutt. The photographer took pictures of all the winners. Lizzie could hardly stand to watch.

"Every single pet here is getting some kind of award," Charles whispered to Lizzie.

"Every pet but ours," she whispered back. How could Sandy ignore Bubbles and Boo, the most adorable, sweetest pets there?

After the last award, and before the applause completely died away, Sandy spoke up again. "Before we part for the day, I do have one more prize to announce, a very special one that the judges and I created on the spot this afternoon. We're calling it the Besties award, and it goes to Bubbles and Boo, who have formed a very special bond."

Lizzie and Charles grinned at each other. Maria whooped and gave Lizzie a high five. "Yes!" said Lizzie. She marched up to Sandy with Charles, Boo, and Bubbles by her side. Sandy knelt to put a medal around Bubbles's neck, then hugged her. She handed Charles another medal and stroked Boo's nose.

"Thank you all for coming," Sandy said to the audience. "I hope to see you all here next year. Oh, and I have one last announcement before we wrap up this very special day." She shot Lizzie a happy glance before she continued. "I didn't have a chance to check about this, so I'm keeping my fingers crossed — but I am hoping to adopt both of these good friends and keep them together for the rest of their lives." She took Boo from Charles's arms and knelt down to kiss Bubbles. The newspaper photographer circled around them, his camera clicking away.

The audience cheered and applauded. Sandy stood up and thanked everyone, and people began to drift off.

Maria jumped up to join Lizzie. "This is awesome!" she said. She threw her arms around Lizzie.

Lizzie shook her head, wondering if she could really believe her ears. She stared at the librarian. "Really?" she asked. "Both of them?"

Sandy nodded. "I've been thinking about it all week. I got interested in rabbits after you came in, and I ended up doing a lot of research about them, mostly online, since you have all our books! Anyway, I decided I'd love to have a bunny."

"What about your boyfriend?" Lizzie asked. "I thought you told us he wasn't an animal person."

"Exactly," said Sandy. "When I heard myself saying that to you last week, I asked myself, 'So why are you with him, then?' We decided we'd be better off as friends, and we broke up. Now I can have all the animals I want! I was going to start off slowly, with just a bunny — but when I heard that Boo and Bubbles needed to stay together, I realized that a pair like that only comes along once in a blue moon. So why not take both?"

Lizzie laughed. "That's great news," she said. "The best news ever." She knew that Bubbles and Boo would be very happy living with Sandy. Now they would be besties forever, just like her and Maria.

PUPPY TIPS

Some dogs get along very well with other types of animals, and some don't. If you already have a dog and you decide to add another pet — like a bunny or a kitten or an iguana — make sure you take the time to introduce the new pet slowly and carefully. You can talk to your vet or do some research at the library or online for some ideas about how to do this. With luck, the two pets will become friends!

Dear Reader,

I don't think my dog, Zipper, would get along very well with a bunny. He really likes to chase things — like balls or squirrels — and I'm afraid he would get a little too excited if a bunny started hopping around the house and doing binkies. If I ever got another pet, it would probably be another dog. Zipper would love to have a dog sister or brother to play with someday — but right now one energetic dog is more than enough for me!

Yours from the Puppy Place,
Ellen Miles

P.S. To see what it was like when Charles and Lizzie fostered a puppy and a kitten together, check out MAGGIE AND MAX!

DON'T MISS THE NEXT PUPPY PLACE ADVENTURE!

Here's a sneak peek at LOLA!

"It's an orphaned wolf pup, howling in the wilderness," said Sammy. He was still being Captain Sam.

"Or a coyote," said David. "Or a prairie dog? Do they make noises?"

Charles shook his head. "It's a dog," he said. He wasn't Captain Charles anymore. He was just Charles again. "And it's not a happy dog. We have to find it." Charles couldn't bear the sound of the dog's howling. He knew a dog did not make that kind of noise unless it was hurting, frightened, or both. Once Buddy had stepped on a thorn that had gone deep into his foot pad. He had whimpered and howled with every step he took until Dad had found the thorn and removed it. Charles had never forgotten that.

"It must be in that settlement to the east," said Sammy, pointing to a distant row of houses whose roofs barely showed through the thick, tall woods. Obviously, Sammy wasn't ready to quit the expeditioning game. "We'll blaze a trail through the forest and rescue the poor animal. Let's go, men!"

Charles leapt over the stream, stepping quickly from rock to rock with David and Sammy close behind him. He plunged into the woods. There was no path, but he pushed through the undergrowth, ignoring the thorns that caught his sleeves and poked his hands. It seemed even darker in the woods; the trees loomed high above them. Charles felt his heart beating faster. What if they got lost in the forest? David had the compass in his backpack, but none of them really knew how to use it. Then he heard the howling again, an urgent screeching sound. "That way!" he said, pointing to the right. "It's coming from that direction." He began to jog, dodging trees and rocks and roots. He didn't even care if David and Sammy were keeping up; he just had to get to that dog.

"Hey, a path!" said David. "Why can't we just go this way?"

Charles turned around. Sure enough, David was right. Charles must have crossed it without seeing it: a well-worn dirt path through the woods. It looked as if some people had cut branches and beat back the brambles, probably to make a trail to the stream.

"It's not an expedition if you take a path," Sammy protested.

"We're not explorers anymore," said Charles. "We just have to find that dog." The whining had not stopped, and Charles couldn't stand to hear it for one second longer. He turned onto the path and began to run now that the way was clear. His backpack bumped and thumped against his back as he galloped down the trail. The screeching sounds of the dog were closer now; they were going in the right direction.

Suddenly, the three boys popped out into the open. They were in a yard, like any other yard: there was a swing set and a shed and a garden bed with a fence around it.

"The settlement!" said Sammy.

"It's just Maple Street," said David.

Charles didn't care whether it was a settlement or a regular neighborhood. He just wanted to find that dog. "This way," he said after listening for a moment. He cut across the yard they were in, then across three others. One had a pool; one had a rock garden; and one had long grass that needed to be mowed. Each yard brought them closer to the crying dog.

"There!" Charles said, pointing to a small pale-blue house that sat at the end of the street. He broke into a run.

A line was strung between the house and a shed in the backyard. Attached to the line was a long wire. And attached to that wire was a dog.

It was a puppy, really. Just a tiny pup, black and white, with an adorable squashed-in face and funny bat ears that stood up when she spotted Charles. For just a moment, she stopped screeching. Then she started again. She ran up and down, whimpering and crying as she zipped back and forth along her line from the house to the shed.

There was a dusty, dry path beneath the line. Charles did not see a food or water bowl or any place for the dog to get out of the weather, other than the shed — but the door to the shed was closed tight. The house was also closed up tight; it was clear that nobody was home.

"This isn't right," he said. He shook his head. "How could anybody leave such a young puppy alone all day?"

David took off his backpack and threw it to the ground. He moved slowly toward the pup, holding out his hand. "It's okay," he said softly. "It's okay, little pup."

Charles's sister, Lizzie, sometimes called David a dog whisperer. He seemed to know just how to talk to dogs and puppies and make them feel safe.

The puppy stopped screeching for a moment. She stopped running up and down. She looked at David, cocking her head.

Can I trust you?

Charles and Sammy took off their backpacks, too. "Poor thing," Sammy said. He finally seemed to have forgotten about being Captain Sam. "What are you doing here all by yourself?" He walked toward the dog. Her ears went back and she took off, zipping up and down her run again.

"Careful," said David. "She's scared."

Charles looked at the blue house again. The shades were drawn and the door was shut tight. Nobody was home.

A distant rumbling came from the heavy gray clouds overhead, and the dog began to whimper again as she raced up and down.

ABOUT THE AUTHOR

Ellen Miles loves dogs, which is why she has a great time writing the Puppy Place books. And guess what? She loves cats, too! (In fact, her very first pet was a beautiful tortoiseshell cat named Jenny.) That's why she came up with the Kitty Corner series. Ellen lives in Vermont and loves to be outdoors with her dog, Zipper, every day, walking, biking, skiing, or swimming, depending on the season. She also loves to read, cook, explore her beautiful state, play with dogs, and hang out with friends and family.

Visit Ellen at www.ellenmiles.net.